T0243139

Wisdom Tooth

BRENDA KAY LONG

AuthorHouse™
1663 Liberty Drive
Bloomington, IN 47403
www.authorhouse.com
Phone: 1 (800) 839-8640

This book is printed on acid-free paper.

ISBN: 978-1-7283-4467-6 (sc)
ISBN: 978-1-7283-4466-9 (e)

Library of Congress Control Number: 2020901444

Print information available on the last page.

Published by AuthorHouse 01/24/2020

authorHOUSE®

Wisdom Tooth

- Easy things that you can do everyday
- Flossing and Brushing chart included

Brenda Kay Long

I'm going to take you on a journey to teach you how to take care of your teeth so that you can have a great smile. Let's go! Follow me. Let's complete the journey......

Mouth Rinsing Monday

Children should rinse their mouths out with a children's mouth rinse. It keeps your mouth feeling fresh and clean. It also tastes great and helps prevent cavities and strengthens your teeth. Don't swallow the mouth rinse and make sure to spit it out!

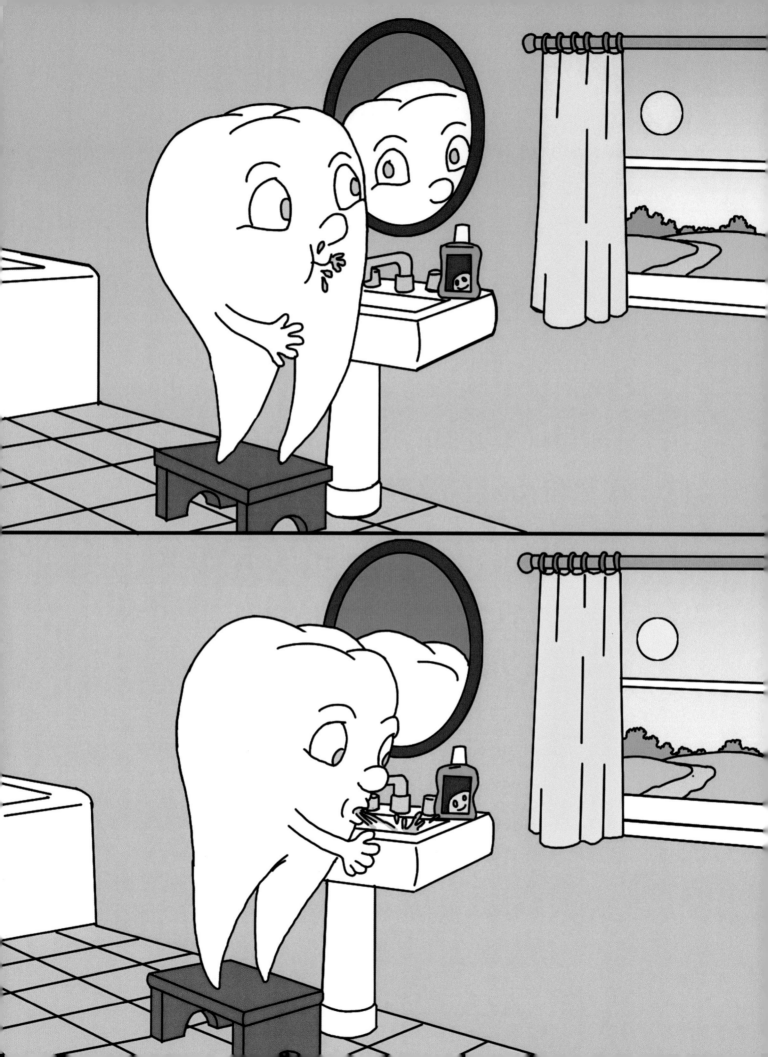

Teeth Brushing Tuesday

Brush your teeth every day. Brush your teeth two times a day both morning and night. Brush your teeth for two minutes.

Brush up and down across and back. Make sure you use a pea sized amount of children's toothpaste on your tooth brush.

When you brush your teeth, you remove food and plaque.

Plaque- The sticky substance that contains bacteria.

Water drinking Wednesday

Drink plenty of water. Water is good for your teeth because it helps to keep them clean. Drinking water also washes away some of the food particles from your teeth that can cause you to have stains and cavities.

Tongue brushing Thursday

Don't forget to brush your tongue. It's important to have a healthy tongue. It's good to have a clean tongue so that your food can taste better.

If you don't brush your teeth, bacteria can grow on it. This bacteria can cause you to have an odor and bugs that will give your breath a not so pleasant smell.

Flossing Friday

Flossing your teeth will help you have healthy gums and teeth gums are what holds your teeth in place.

Children should start flossing their teeth between the ages of two and six. Children should floss their teeth once a day.

Flossing gets rid of plaque between your teeth that is difficult or impossible to reach with a toothbrush.

Don't forgot to take care of your teeth every day including Saturdays and Sundays with all of these tasks I've shown you on this journey. Now, let's get started on having a healthy mouth and teeth so that you can have a great smile.

Flossing Chart

Brushing Chart

17

Things you should know

- Change your toothbrush every three to four months.

- Use a soft bristle toothbrush.

- Throw your toothbrush away after a cold. If you have an electric toothbrush, change the brush heads.

- You should visit your dentist two times a year.

Healthy Fruits and Vegetables

- Apples
- Bananas
- Celery
- Carrots
- Cheese
- Leafy Greens

MOUTH CHART

Born and raised in Skippers Virginia.
Brenda later moved to Washington
D.C. with her mother and four siblings.
After attending high school at Frank W.
Ballou Senior high she later continued
her studies at Georgetown School of

Science and Arts, where she received her degree in Dental Assisting. After graduating she immediately began her career in the dental field working along side with Dr. Stephen I. Barsky.

Brenda believes that dental care is a part of healthcare and uses education to encourage children and adults to take care of their teeth. She has facilitated workshops at various schools across the District of Colombia area in honor of National Children's Dental Health Month providing students with advice on proper teeth care. Brenda is currently married with four children and resides in Washington D.C. working as a Licensed Dental Assistant.